Beach Toys vs. School Supplies

Mike Ciccotello

Farrar Straus Giroux
New York

To my dear wife, Anne-Marie, who builds

an awesome pillow fort

Farrar Straus Giroux Books for Young Readers · An imprint of Macmillan Publishing Group, LLC · 120 Broadway, New York, NY, 10271

Copyright © 2021 by Mike Ciccotello · All rights reserved · Color separations by Embassy Graphics · Printed in China by Hung Hing Off-set Printing
Co. Ltd., Heshan City, Guangdong Province · Designed by Mercedes Padró · First edition, 2021 · 10 9 8 7 6 5 4 3 2 1

mackids.com

Library of Congress Cataloging-in-Publication Data · Names: Ciccotello, Mike, author, illustrator. · Title: Beach toys vs. school supplies / Mike
Ciccotello. · Other titles: Beach toys versus school supplies · Description: First edition. | New York : Farrar Straus Giroux Books for Young Readers,
2021. | Summary: When Shovel sees Ruler at the beach, he knows there will be trouble but a sandcastle-building contest proves surprising to both
the Beach Toys and the School Supplies. · Identifiers: LCCN 2020005701 | ISBN 9780374314040 (hardcover) · Subjects: CYAC: Toys—Fiction. |
Office equipment and supplies—Fiction. | Sandcastles—Fiction. | Contests—Fiction. | Cooperativeness—Fiction. | Beaches—Fiction. · Classification:
LCC PZ7.1.C553 Be 2021 | DDC [E]—dc23

Our books may be purchased in bulk for promotional, educational, or business use. Please contact your local bookseller or the Macmillan Corporate
and Premium Sales Department at (800) 221-7945 ext. 5442 or by email at MacmillanSpecialMarkets@macmillan.com.

On the day that would be remembered as the Big Showdown, Shovel was lying on the beach, minding his own business, when a strange shadow blocked his sun.

He looked up and saw. . . Ruler?

Shovel shook his head. He must have had sand in his eyes.

But, no, it was his smart-aleck old rival—making his mark on Shovel's beach.

And before Labor Day, too.

"What are you doing here?" asked Shovel.

"Working," Ruler replied.
"School starts next week.
I wanted to survey my skills."

"You school supplies are all the same," Shovel said, getting a dig in. "Work, work, work! When do you have any fun?"

Ruler rolled his eyes and checked the height of a lifeguard chair. "Fun is overrated. Learning is far superior to playing silly beach games. School rules! Get it?"

"You think you're so clever," Shovel huffed. "Why don't we settle this once and for all. With a contest—a sandcastle-building contest."

Ruler jumped down and inched over. "Just what I was hoping you'd say!" He called to his friends, "Hey, everybody, we've got ourselves a showdown!"

The beach toys watched as the rest of the school supplies made their way down the boardwalk.

"We're totally going to deflate them," said Beach Ball.

"Don't hold your breath," said Swim Mask. "Maybe they have some skills."

"Not a chance," Shovel said with a laugh. "We're going to bury them."

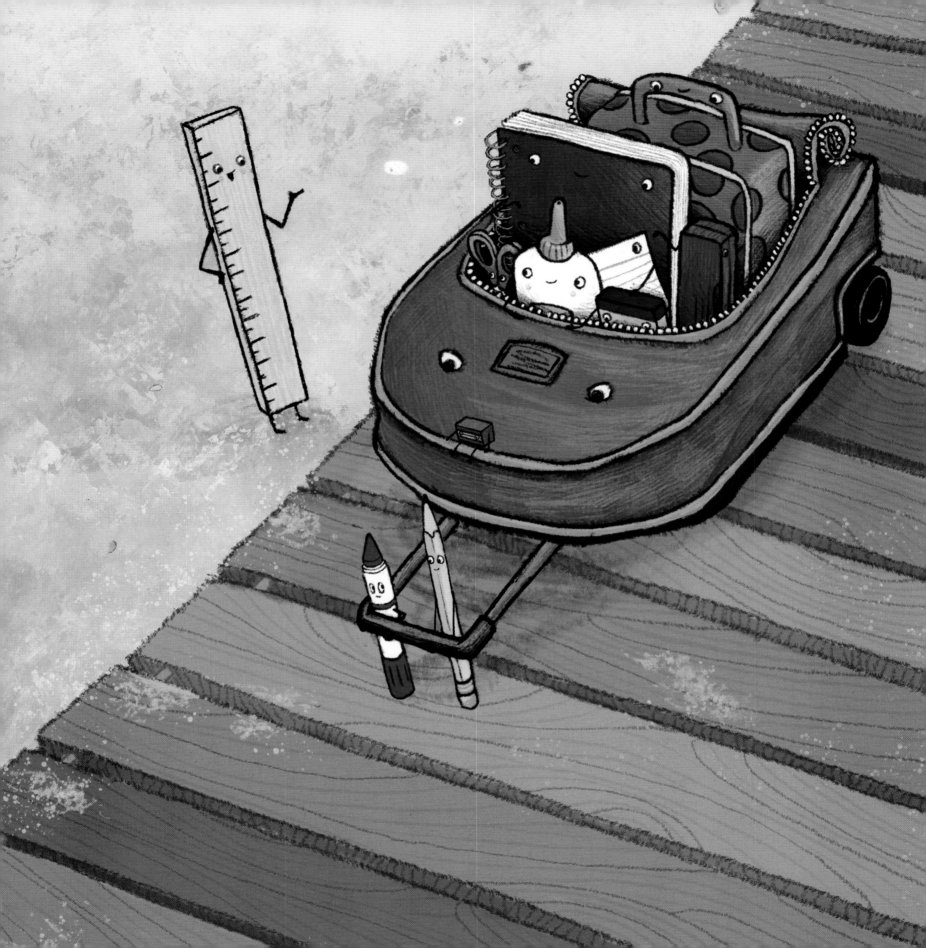

"Sounds like you could use my help," said Whistle.

The beach toys and school supplies gathered around.

"*Tweet!*" blasted the referee. "You'll have one hour to build your sandcastles. Now, it's best to consider the location because of the—"

"Yeah, yeah . . . we know what we're doing,"
Scissors cut in. "Thanks, Tweetie."

Whistle blew off the rude comment.
"Let the contest begin!"

The beach toys scouted a location far from the school supplies—and far from the water. Then they started doing what they did best.

Hoe and Rake flattened out the sand.

Shovel dug the moat while
Bucket fetched water.

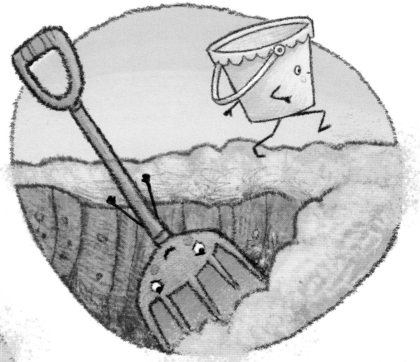

Castle and her kids went to
town building, well, a town.

The whole time they worked, the beach toys laughed, told jokes, and sang songs.

The school supplies, on the other hand, were completely silent—like they were studying or something. This made Shovel nervous. He wanted to take a peek at how their castle was coming along, but he knew that he should keep his eyes on his own work.

As the sun rose higher in the sky, the beach toys scurried to add their finishing touches. Shovel thought the castle looked fantastic. It might have been their best one all summer!

He was sure they had won the contest. So when Whistle tweeted that time was up, Shovel started cheering before he even turned around and saw— *Gasp!*

Maybe their best wasn't good enough, after all.

"Behold, our castle of classrooms!" said Scissors, a real cutup.

"A palace of learning," pointed out Pencil.

"We've gobbled up a thing or two about construction from the library," said Lunch Box.
"Take note!" shouted Index Card.

Ruler towered over Shovel. "I think it's clear who stands out today," he said.

Shovel sank into the sand. Why couldn't he have kept his big mouth shut? For once, he just wanted to prove that beach toys could outsmart school supplies. But he had failed.

"*TWEET! TWEET!*" Whistle sounded the alarm. "Unfortunately, you school supplies didn't want to hear the number-one rule of sandcastle building: DON'T BUILD TOO CLOSE TO THE WATER!"

Sure enough, the tide had turned. Waves were creeping closer and closer. The winners' masterpiece was doomed!

Ruler and the school supplies panicked and lined up in front of their castle, which was a terrible idea. Notebook would get waterlogged. Pencil would be erased. And Glue would never be able to stick to her position.

"Maybe we should lend a hand," Bucket suggested.

"Are you kidding?" Shovel said. "Why should we help them?"

Beach Ball said what the others were thinking. "Because it's no fun watching anyone's castle get knocked over by a wave. And we are all about fun, remember?"

Shovel had to admit that was true. "Well, how can we save them now, even if we wanted to?"

Everyone looked at him. He was the master moat-digger, after all.
"Fine," mumbled Shovel, "but the only way we have a chance is
if we all work together."

Shovel led his beach toys to the front line, where they showed their rivals what to do.

As high tide approached, everyone got busy digging a moat

and building other defenses as fast as they could.

The waves didn't stand a chance. They washed harmlessly against the walls and into the moat. The water drained away safely.

"Hooray!" everyone cheered.

This time, it was Ruler's turn for a change of heart. "That was some quick thinking, Shovel," he admitted. "You and your friends really measure up."

"And we really dig your castle," Shovel said. "I guess you do know how to let loose and have fun after all—in your own way."

"We do," said Ruler, "but it was even more fun when we did it together. Hey! Are you thinking what I'm thinking?"

Shovel smiled. Then they both shouted the same thing.

With their rivalry forgotten, the day of the Big Showdown turned into a beach-party celebration of new friendships that would last for countless school years and summers to come.

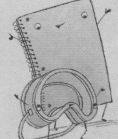